A Note to Parents and Caregivers:

Read-it! Readers are for children who are just starting on the amazing road to reading. These beautiful books support both the acquisition of reading skills and the love of books.

The RED LEVEL presents familiar topics using common words and repeating sentence patterns.

The BLUE LEVEL presents new ideas using a larger vocabulary and varied sentence structure.

The YELLOW LEVEL presents more challenging ideas, a broad vocabulary, and wide variety in sentence structure.

The GREEN LEVEL presents more complex ideas, an extended vocabulary range, and expanded language structures.

When sharing a book with your child, read in short stretches, pausing often to talk about the pictures. Have your child turn the pages and point to the pictures and familiar words. And be sure to reread favorite stories or parts of stories.

There is no right or wrong way to share books with children. Find time to read with your child, and pass on the legacy of literacy.

Adria F. Klein, Ph.D.
Professor Emeritus
California State University
San Bernardino, California

Editor: Bob Temple
Creative Director: Terri Foley
Editorial Adviser: Andrea Cascardi
Copy Editor: Laurie Kahn
Designer: Melissa Voda
Page production: The Design Lab
The illustrations in this book were rendered in pastels.

Picture Window Books
5115 Excelsior Boulevard
Suite 232
Minneapolis, MN 55416
1-877-845-8392
www.picturewindowbooks.com

Printed in the United States of America.

Library of Congress Cataloging-in-Publication Data
White, Mark, 1971–
The fox and the grapes : a retelling of Aesop's fable / written by Mark White ;
illustrated by Sara Rojo.
p. cm. — (Read-it! readers fairy tales)
Summary: Retells the fable of a frustrated fox that, after many tries to reach
a high bunch of grapes, decides they must be sour anyway.
ISBN 1-4048-0218-5
[1. Folklore. 2. Fables.] I. Aesop. II. Rojo, Sara, 1973– ill. III. Title. IV. Series.
PZ8.2.W55Fo 2004
398.24'529775—dc21   2003006303

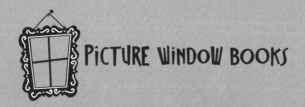

The Fox and the Grapes
A Retelling of Aesop's Fable

Written by Mark White

Illustrated by Sara Rojo

Bel Air
Library Adviser:
Former Coordinator of Children's Services
Anoka County (Minnesota) Library

Reading Advisers:
Adria F. Klein, Ph.D.
Professor Emeritus, California State University
San Bernardino, California

Susan Kesselring, M.A.
Literacy Educator
Rosemount-Apple Valley-Eagan (Minnesota) School District

Picture Window Books
Minneapolis, Minnesota

There was once a vineyard
upon a hill.

One day, a hungry fox
walked among the tall posts

where the grapevines grew.

The fox looked up
at the juicy, ripe grapes.
His mouth began to water.

10

The fox jumped high
and snapped his jaws.
He bit nothing but air.

The fox tried again.

He took a running start
and leaped at the grapes.

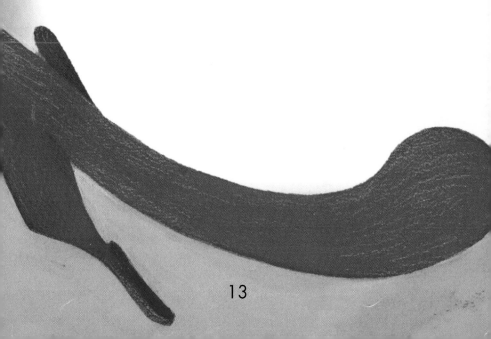

Once again, he came crashing down
before reaching the ripe fruit.

How could he reach those grapes?

The fox tried to climb the thick posts
that held up the vines.

His paws weren't made for climbing.
Once again, the fox fell to the ground.

20

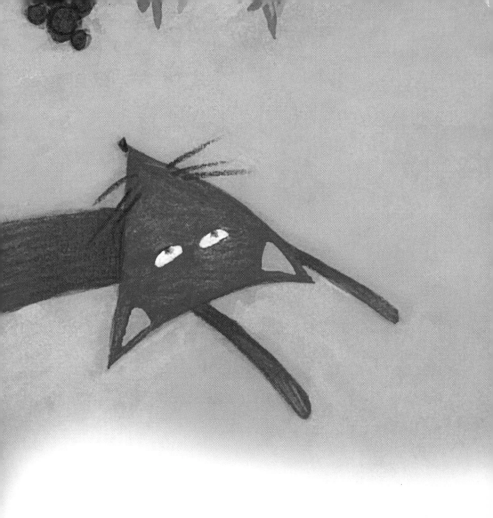

The fox rested to catch his breath.
Then he gave one last mighty leap.

He still couldn't reach the grapes.
Finally, he decided to give up.

The fox walked away.

"Those grapes are probably
sour anyway," he said to himself.

The fox knew the grapes were tasty.
It made him feel better to pretend
they were sour, because he couldn't
have them.